Mr. Linguini's Favourite

Little Naptime Stories for Girls and Boys

By
Lady Hershey for
Her Little Brother Mr. Linguini

ISBN 978-1-7770569-2-6

For information: www.sleep-cozy.ca or www.sleep-cozy.org

First edition
Published in Canada

Table of contents

Introduction

I'm so happy you chose to read my book of little naptime stories. Maybe some of you already know me and my little brother from my other books, *Sleep Cozy* and *Who's Dwindle?* If not, I would like to happily introduce myself.

My name is Lady Hershey, and I have a little brother named Mr. Linguini. Mr. Linguini never used to like taking afternoon naps, until I wrote him little naptime stories. Now he can't wait to hear them, and he takes his naps every afternoon without making a fuss.

Mr. Linguini believes stories are magical. When he wakes up from his cozy little naptime, he feels refreshed and ready to take on the afternoon.

We would like to share these stories with you, so you can wake up full of fresh energy, too, just like Mr. Linguini does. Go get your favourite stuffed animal (Mr. Linguini's favourite stuffed animal is named Balloons), make yourself cozy, and enjoy our little book of naptime stories.

> Love,
> Lady Hershey and Mr. Linguini
> Cherish each day

**Other books by Lady Hershey
for her Little Brother Mr. Linguini**

Sleep Cozy – Little Bedtime Stories for Girls and Boys

Who's Dwindle? Little Christmas Stories for Girls and Boys

Whoo Hoo Hoo! Little Everyday Stories for Girls and Boys

The Teddy Bear

"Mommy, could you read me a bedtime story?" asked Harpreet.

"Sure I can," her mommy said. "But this time, I will tell you a special story that comes right from my heart."

Harpreet ran to go get her favourite teddy bear, named Kangaroo. She held him tightly in her little arms as she cuddled up beside her mommy, ready to listen to the story.

"Are you ready, Harpreet?"

"Yes, mommy."

"This is how the story goes. Once upon a time, there was a young lady named Sandy, who really wanted a beautiful baby girl. She travelled very far away to find her, and she instantly fell in love with her as soon as she saw her beautiful face. She was like an angel. Sandy held the baby tightly in her arms and gave her a little teddy bear, and couldn't wait to bring her home so they could be a forever family together."

"Where did Sandy go to get the little baby?" asked Harpreet.

"She went all the way to India," her mommy said.

"What else happened?"

"As the little baby girl was growing up, her mommy would tell her about adoption."

"You talk about adoption. But what does that really mean?" Harpreet asked.

"Well, there are many reasons for it," said Harpreet's mommy. "But for this little baby girl in the story, it meant that her birth mommy loved her very much but could not take care of her. She gave her up to someone like Sandy, who could give her a beautiful, glorious, happy life, full of opportunities."

"What was the baby's name?" Harpreet asked.

"Harpreet."

"That's my name! And yours is Sandy! The story is about me, and Kangaroo is the teddy bear you gave me. I'm adopted! I love you, mommy!"

"I love you more!" said Harpreet's mommy. "And one day when you're older, I will take you to visit India, so you can learn about where you were born."

Harpreet gave her mommy the biggest hug ever, and her mommy hugged her right back. They hugged so tightly that they felt each others' hearts beat.

Doggie Snow Angels

One snowy winter afternoon, a little boy named Oren couldn't wait to go outside to the backyard to play in the snow. His Husky dog, Chickpea, was also excited.

Chickpea loved the snow, and he especially loved to play with Oren and make snow angels together.

That afternoon, Chickpea noticed a squirrel sitting on a frozen chestnut tree branch. The squirrel looked cold and hungry. Chickpea didn't notice the cold very much, because Huskies have lots of fur to keep them warm. He felt bad for the little creature, and tugged Oren's winter coat to show him the squirrel.

The squirrel slowly came down the frozen tree branch and noticed Chickpea's doggie snow angels in the snow. Even though Chickpea was a big dog, the squirrel thought that he had to be friendly.

The squirrel reached the snow-covered ground, and noticed that, in making doggie snow angels, Chickpea had uncovered chestnuts that had fallen from the chestnut tree, and had been buried by the snow.

Chickpea was a loving doggie, and he helped gather a bunch of chestnuts. Oren helped him leave them in a pile for the squirrel. The squirrel was very happy. He ate one of the chestnuts, then brought the rest back to his nest.

"I love you, Chickpea," said Oren. "You're a good, kind, and gentle doggie. Even that little squirrel thinks so."

When they had finished playing and went back inside, Oren made sure that Chickpea got his favourite treat. That day, Oren was inspired to become more thoughtful and giving, all because of a big, beautiful, warm-hearted doggie named Chickpea, who loved making doggie snow angels.

A Beautiful Heart

There once was a boy named Tommi, who was selfless and would put everyone else before himself, especially his little sister Rosemary.

One afternoon, Tommi heard his mommy tell her friend, "I wish I could put Rosemary in swimming lessons, but for now, I just can't afford it."

Tommi knew how hard his mommy worked, but they still did not have much money. He ran to his room to get his piggybank, and he brought it to his mommy.

"This is for your wish, mommy. It will help put Rosemary in swimming lessons."

"You have a beautiful heart, Tommi," said his mommy, "but I know how long you have been saving for a guitar."

Tommi was so selfless that he would not take no for an answer. Rosemary got to take swimming lessons, with the help of Tommi's piggybank money.

A couple of days later, Tommi's grandpa was cleaning his attic and found his old guitar, which had been hidden away for years. Tommi was very happy.

"Thank you," he said. "I love it even more because it was yours. How did you know I wanted a guitar?"

"I didn't," said Grandpa.

"Wow!" said Tommi. "Then it really is true that when you do good things for others, good things happen to you."

Tommi's mommy looked at her little boy with great joy. "I wish there were more Tommies in the world," she thought to herself.

Holy Ravioli! Where Did Your Teeth Go?

Hi, Dasha!" Flynn said excitedly, with a smile from ear to ear. He hoped his little sister, who was four years old, would notice that he had lost two of his front baby teeth at once. Dasha noticed right away.

"Holy ravioli!" she shouted. "Where did your teeth go?"

"What do you mean, where did my teeth go?" Flynn asked. "They fell out. They were my baby teeth. Everyone loses their baby teeth. It means I'm getting bigger. You will lose your baby teeth one day, too."

Dasha started crying. "How are we going to get them back? Or are they gone forever?" she sobbed.

"Our forever teeth grow in," explained Flynn. "And our forever teeth will not fall out, as long as we brush, floss, and visit the dentist."

Dasha still cried a little while longer, but stopped when she realized how happy Flynn was to have lost his baby teeth.

I already put them under my pillow," Flynn said proudly. "I'm going to get double the coins from the Tooth Fairy."

"How do I know when my baby teeth will fall out?" asked Dasha.

"They are going to start to wiggle and wobble," Flynn said.

"Wiggle and wobble?"

"Yup, wiggle and wobble!"

They both laughed and laughed.

Flynn looked cute when he smiled with his front baby teeth missing. Dasha now was happy, too, because she had learned that losing your baby teeth meant that you're getting bigger, and will get a lot of coins from the Tooth Fairy.

So, So Adorable

Once upon a time, there was a little girl named Jenny. Jenny was so shy that it was difficult for her to make friends.

One day, everything changed. Jenny's daddy came home with two pot-bellied piglets. Jenny was thrilled. She named the piglets Squiggly and Curly. They were full of life, and so, so adorable.

Squiggly was white with black spots, and Curly was black with white spots. Squiggly and Curly loved when Jenny gave them belly rubs and read little stories to them, and they both loved to join in with her when she danced.

Jenny had a big backyard, and the piglets loved to run around, chasing Jenny and playing ball. Jenny's shyness began to slowly fade away. Soon she started making friends who really liked her for who she was, and they loved to listen to her talk about her pet piglets.

On her sixth birthday, Jenny invited her friends over to her house for a party. There were balloons, fun games to play, and a lot of treats to share. Suddenly, Squiggly and Curly came running out, excitedly oinking and oinking at Jenny's friends.

"They are so, so adorable!" Jenny's friends said.

All it took was two little baby pot-bellied piglets to take away Jenny's shyness, and give her the confidence she needed to be her adorable self.

Oink, oink!

Mira, Short for Miracle

What is a miracle?" Mira asked her mommy.

"You're a miracle," her mommy answered. "I fell in love with you when you were in my tummy." This made Mira very happy.

"Are you a miracle, mommy?" she asked.

"Of course," replied her mommy, "and so is everyone else in the world."

"Are all the puppies and kittens a miracle, too?" asked Mira.

"Of course," said her mommy.

"Wow!" said Mira. "Just like the caterpillar that turns into a butterfly?"

"That's a colourful miracle," said Mira's mommy. "And let's not forget the pretty flowers, and the way the leaves on the trees change colour with the seasons. Those are colourful miracles, too. And when we see a colourful rainbow in the sky, that's a reminder that miracles are real. Do you know why I named you Mira?"

"Why, mommy?"

"Because Mira is short for miracle, and I love my little miracle."

"I love you more, mommy," said Mira. "Love is the biggest miracle."

"It sure is," said her mommy.

Me and My Cool Wheels!

One day, a little boy named Hendrix was practicing throwing his basketball into a net at the playground.

"Hey! Can I play, too?" shouted Cooper, who was new to the neighbourhood. "I love playing basketball."

"But you're in a wheelchair," said Hendrix.

"I know!" said Cooper. "Aren't my wheels cool? Don't baby me just because I'm in a wheelchair. I'll even let you go first."

"Okay, you can play," said Hendrix.

Hendrix got three baskets in a row, and then it was Cooper's turn. Cooper got eight baskets in a row.

"Wow! You're good!" said Hendrix.

"I know," said Cooper. "I'll be in the Special Olympics one day with my cool wheels."

"I'm going to be in the Olympics, too," said Hendrix. "Why don't we practice together, so we can both become great?"

The boys gave each other a high-five.

That same day, when Hendrix went home, he sat on his daddy's office chair, which had wheels. Right away, he thought of Cooper and his cool wheels, and how no wheelchair would stop his dreams from coming true, as long as he had passion for the game and practiced hard at it.

Cooper and Hendrix became great pals and amazing basketball players, and had lots of fun practicing against each other.

A Cat and a Mouse

There once was a cat named Chito. Chito liked to chase a mouse that lived in his house. The mouse would run and run, and Chito thought the game was fun. Chito would chase the mouse all over the house.

Chito knew that the mouse liked cheese. Chito would always find a way to leave some cheese on the kitchen floor, so the mouse would come out from its hiding place. But as the mouse came out and smelled the cheese, Chito would chase the mouse away. The mouse would always escape through a little tiny hole in the wall, and would end up in the backyard.

One day, Chito looked out the window and could see the mouse outside. He saw a big outdoor cat walk into the garden, getting ready to catch the mouse. That was the first time Chito saw the fear in the mouse's eyes. The mouse was shaking and had little tears running down his cheeks. Chito felt sad for the little mouse, and until that moment, he did not understand how scared and helpless the mouse really was.

The outdoor cat chased the little mouse with all his might, but luckily the mouse made it through his hole and into the house. When the mouse got back inside, there was a fresh piece of cheese on the kitchen floor, but this time, Chito just sat there, purring happily, and let the mouse enjoy his cheese in peace.

From that day on, Chito and the little mouse became best friends, and Chito always protected and fed the mouse, and never scared him again.

That is the story of a cat and a mouse.

Fancy Clothes Don't Make Me!

This is a story of a little girl named Moya, who was confident and happy. When Moya laughed, she could get everyone to laugh along with her. Moya did not care about fancy clothes, like her friends did. They would even make fun of her for what she wore, and sometimes they would ask her where she got her old clothes.

"They were my big sister's clothes," Moya would tell them proudly.

"And why do you wear that raggedy old hat?" they asked one day.

"This hat was not my grandpa's, but my great-grandpa's hat," she replied. "It's very special."

"It looks so old," they told her.

"But it means a lot to me because it's old," Moya replied, full of confidence. "Fancy clothes don't make me. I make the clothes!"

Moya's friends would have never dared to wear the sort of clothes Moya wore.

But one day, Moya's friends were at her house, playing in the backyard. Suddenly, the sprinkler turned on, and Moya's friends all got soaked. Their fancy clothes got wet, and they were not at all happy about it.

"You can wear some of my clothes," said Moya.

"No way!" they said.

"Just until your clothes dry," Moya promised. Her friends agreed and put on the dry clothes

To their amazement, they felt more relaxed and very comfortable. They ran and played, and did not have to worry that they were going to get dirty.

"This is the most fun we've ever had!" they told Moya. They laughed and laughed.

"See!" said Moya. "Fancy clothes don't make you. You make the clothes!"

The next day at school, Moya's friends did not have their usual fancy clothes on. Instead, they wore their plain and comfortable clothes, and they seemed more confident in themselves. What Moya said was true. They had learned that fancy clothes don't make you. You make the clothes.

Thank You, Papa!

Once upon a time, there was a little girl named Della, who was born deaf. Della could not hear the bells ringing, birds chirping, or anything else. Della was very happy with herself the way she was, and she was happy with the life she had. It did not bother her that she could not hear.

Della loved her Papa. He would tell her that she could accomplish anything that she put her mind to. Della's Papa always gave her lots of attention, and would leave her encouraging little notes to read.

Della and her Papa learned sign language together. Sometimes Della would tell her Papa, "That's enough, Papa. You sign too much." But Della knew her Papa was just happy to be able to speak with her using sign language.

One day, Della wanted to show her Papa how much she loved him, so she wrote him a little poem, and it went like this:

Papa, you make me so happy,

even when I'm taking a nappy,

because you're my pappy.

Thank You, Papa!

Della's Papa gave her a big gigantic hug.

"You are my little miracle baby girl," he said.

Moo-Moo and Quack-Quack

Once upon a time, there was a little boy named Alfredo. Alfredo's family lived on a farm, and Alfredo had lots of fun with the farm animals, especially Moo-Moo the cow and Quack-Quack the duck.

On his seventh birthday, Alfredo got his first video game console. At first, he was only allowed to play with it for one hour a day, but as the days went by, he convinced his parents to let him spend many hours a day playing video games.

Alfredo's mommy and daddy were kind and loving. They always spoke softly to him, and always made time for him. But when Alfredo started playing video games, he stopped listening to his parents, and sometimes even ignored them. This made them very sad.

One day, as Alfredo was about to sit down to play a video game, he heard Moo-Moo and Quack-Quack making lots of noise outside his bedroom window. Moo-Moo was mooing and mooing, and Quack-Quack was quacking and quacking. They were both looking straight at Alfredo through the window as they mooed and quacked.

Alfredo ran outside.

"What's going on?" he asked his animal friends.

Quack-Quack went straight to the kiddie pool and splashed water on Alfredo and Moo-Moo. That's when Alfredo realized his friends needed attention, too.

"I'm sorry, guys," he said. "I miss you, too."

Alfredo realized that too much of anything is not good, and that includes fun things, like video games.

Now when Alfredo's mommy and daddy call him, he always answers them and pays attention to what they have to say. Alfredo only plays one hour of video games a day, and spends the rest of his playtime outside in the fresh air with his friends Moo-Moo and Quack-Quack.

Ugly Should Not Be a Word

"I don't like the word ugly," declared Marcia. "It even sounds ugly."

"What's wrong?" asked her daddy. "Why are you upset?"

"My friend Anita said Nana Phoebe is ugly and that she looks like a big raisin."

"I don't blame you for being upset," said Marcia's daddy. "Ugly should not be a word. Your Nana is a beautiful person, and every line on her face tells a story."

"I don't see Nana Phoebe as old," said Marcia. "I just see my beautiful Nana that I love and adore. I don't like the word ugly! We can't all like the same thing, but if you don't like something, that doesn't mean that it's ugly. That goes for people, too."

When Marcia saw her friend Anita the next day, she noticed that Anita looked very sad. Marcia was a kind and loving little girl, and even though Anita hurt her feelings about her Nana Phoebe, Marcia still asked Anita what was wrong.

"Someone said I have an ugly nose," cried Anita.

"I really don't like the word ugly," said Marcia. "It should not be a word! I love your nose and I think it's cute, because it's part of you."

Anita smiled. "I'm sorry I called your Nana ugly," she said.

It was then that Anita understood that we all see things differently, and also wished that ugly was not a word. Nobody is ugly.

My Umbrella Came Back

It was a rainy afternoon, and a little girl named Mary was walking home hand-in-hand with her Nana Grace. They each held their umbrellas in their other hand. Mary loved her little purple polka dot umbrella that her Nana Grace had given to her on her fifth birthday.

When they got home, Mary left her umbrella open on the front porch to dry, next to Nana Grace's umbrella, which was closed. As soon as they stepped inside, Mary looked out the window and saw a gust of wind blow away her open umbrella.

"My umbrella! The wind blew it away!" Mary shouted. "It's flying away in the sky, Nana! Nana, what are we going to do?"

Nana Grace tried to reassure Mary, but Mary started to cry.

"These things happen," said Nana Grace. "It's okay. I will buy you another umbrella."

"But I love that umbrella," Mary said. "I don't want a new one!"

Mary looked out the window and up at the sky. "Please, wind, bring my umbrella back!" she said. But her little umbrella had been carried off by the wind and was nowhere to be seen.

That night, Mary went to bed believing and hoping that the wind had heard her wish.

The next morning, Mary looked out the front window, and there it was! Her little purple polka dot umbrella was resting on the lawn. She could not have been happier.

"My umbrella came back!" she said with joy. "Thank you, wind! I had faith in you to blow it back, and you did!"

Some Things Are Just Impossible to Stop!

It was Saturday night, and a little girl named Flora was very tired and sleepy. She stretched out her arms and gave a big yawn. Flora then noticed that her puppy named Marty and her kitten named Ollie were yawning, too. She thought her pets looked unbelievably adorable as they yawned.

Flora yawned again, and so did Marty and Ollie. Now all three of them were yawning at once, and they couldn't stop. Flora's mommy, daddy, and Grandma Jo-Jo suddenly started yawning, too.

"I can't believe we're all yawning together," said Flora's mommy.

"I can't stop yawning," said Flora. "Grandma Jo-Jo, you look funny and cute when you yawn."

"I can't stop!" said Grandma Jo-Jo.

"Some things are just impossible to stop, and you can't stop a yawn," said Flora's daddy.

The whole family went to bed yawning.

"One day when I grow up, I'm going to be a scientist," Flora thought to herself as she was falling asleep. "Then I'll find out why you can't stop a yawn. In the meantime, it's fun to see everyone yawning at the same time."

Yawning is like magic! Once you start, everyone else yawns, too, and you yawn even more with your family and pets.

Did You Do Your Homework?

"Did you do your homework?" little Pixel asked his older brother, Dudley.

"Not yet, but I will soon," Dudley replied.

"You must!" Pixel reminded him. "You know we can't go anywhere until you finish your homework."

"I will," said Dudley. "I really want to go to the car show with Daddy on Sunday, but he said we can't go if I don't finish my homework."

"How is your homework coming along?" asked Dudley's daddy.

"I am going to do it first thing Saturday morning," Dudley replied confidently.

"You should just do it now," said Pixel. "Then you can be sure you'll get it done."

"I have all day tomorrow. I'll do it then," Dudley promised. "You don't understand, Pixel. You're still little, and you're lucky that you don't get homework in kindergarten."

Saturday passed and Dudley still had not touched his homework. Pixel started to feel worried and annoyed, because he really wanted to go to the car show on Sunday. So Pixel took Dudley's math homework and tried to do it for him, but because he was still little, all he managed to do was scribble all over the page.

Sunday morning arrived, and Pixel told Dudley that he had done all his homework for him. Dudley was thrilled to not have to do his homework after all.

When their daddy asked if Dudley had done his homework, Dudley said, "Yes."

Because their daddy was also excited to go to the car show, he forgot to check to make sure Dudley's homework was correct. They had a lot of fun together at the car show, and Dudley thought he didn't need to worry about his homework any more.

The next day at school, Dudley proudly turned in his homework.

"What is this scribbling?" asked Miss Gitty as she read Dudley's homework. "How could one plus one equal a happy face, and why are the rest of the questions answered with little pictures of trucks and cars?"

Miss Gitty called Dudley and Pixel's daddy, and that night, both boys got a timeout.

"This is what happens when you don't do your homework!" Pixel said.

Dudley was afraid he would have to go back to kindergarten with Pixel. From then on, Dudley always did his own homework, and he always finished it on time.

Three Little Raindrops

There once was a boy named Raymond who had a negative attitude. His negativity made his big sister Ama upset.

"Raymond, stop being so negative!" she would always say.

"Leave me alone!" Raymond shouted back one day. He went out to the backyard and sat on a lawn chair, being his grumpy self.

Suddenly, a little raindrop landed on Raymond's cheek, and he ran inside.
"It's starting to rain!" he shouted.

"No, it's not," said Ama. "The sun is shining, and there are no clouds in the sky."

Raymond went back outside and sat on the lawn chair again. He soon felt another raindrop land on his cheek. Raymond ran back inside.

"It is starting to rain!" he shouted again.

"No, it's not," said Ama. "There is no rain anywhere."

"Come outside and see it for yourself," said Raymond.

Raymond and Ama each went outside and sat on a lawn chair. Ama enjoyed the sunshine, but Raymond was still grumpy.

"See!" Raymond shouted again. "See, Ama! Another raindrop! Now that's three little raindrops!"

"Don't be silly," Ama replied. "That's the neighbour's sprinkler. They're watering their grass today. You thought the worst because you're always negative and grumpy."

Raymond felt silly. He thought about what Ama said, and from then on, he tried to be more positive. And what do you know! Raymond became much happier, which made Ama happier, too.

Whenever Raymond felt a little negative, he remembered the three little raindrops that landed on his cheek. He believed it must have been his Fairy Godmother that sent them, to remind him that being positive is one of the keys to happiness.

"A-goo, goo-goo!"

"A-goo, goo-goo!" said six-year-old Joel to his baby sister Bernadette. Bernadette was sitting in her high chair, playing with her new toy rattle.

"A-goo, goo-goo!" Joel said again. He made funny faces and funny noises.

Baby Bernadette loved the attention from Joel. She was always full of joy whenever Joel played with her, and she would try to make funny faces just like her big brother.

Baby Bernadette got so excited that she dropped her rattle on the floor, but Joel quickly picked it up, smiling happily. Then, baby Bernadette threw the rattle again, and Joel picked it up again. Baby Bernadette had quickly learned that every time she dropped her rattle, Joel would pick it up and give it back to her.

"Here you go!" Joel said each time he picked up the rattle, and baby Bernadette would happily throw it back down onto the floor.

This went on for a while. Joel was now tired, but baby Bernadette was so happy that she did not want to stop. Luckily, Griffin, the family's dog, picked up the rattle from the floor and took it to her playpen in another room. But baby Bernadette did not make a fuss. As it turned out, she was tired, too.

"I love you, baby Bernadette," said Joel. "Aren't new discoveries fun?"

"A-goo, goo-goo," laughed baby Bernadette, and she made a funny face, just like Joel's.

Fluffy Wuffy, What a Cat!

Fluffy Wuffy was a cat who liked to sleep on the front door mat. Fluffy Wuffy was not a very nice cat, and he would hiss at everybody who passed by the house.

One day, Fluffy Wuffy chased away a skunk from the house, and the skunk sprayed him. Fluffy Wuffy smelled so bad that he was not allowed to sleep on the front door mat. No one wanted to go near him.

Thankfully, even though Fluffy Wuffy was a mean cat, his owner cared about him very much, and they took him to the vet. The vet gave Fluffy Wuffy a buzz cut and a bath, which Fluffy Wuffy didn't like very much at all. For a while after that, Fluffy Wuffy wasn't even very fluffy.

Fluffy Wuffy then became a nice cat. He does not hiss anymore, and he certainly will not chase skunks again. Now he likes sleeping on the inside door mat, and greets his owner's visitors with a purr and a happy meow.

Fluffy Wuffy, what a cat!

I Love You More Than French Fries

There once was a little girl named Nola, who had a best friend named Bexley. One day, Nola and Bexley stopped being friends over something silly. Nola was upset because Bexley had eaten her candy without asking. Bexley said she was sorry, but Nola did not forgive her. This made Bexley very sad.

On that very same day, while Nola's family was having dinner, Nola snuck a French fry from her little brother, Stevo. Stevo loves French fries, but he was not mad at Nola. He just looked at her and smiled for a moment.

Then he whispered in her ear, "I love you more than French fries."

Nola smiled back at her brother and thought of Bexley.

"Love is forgiving, and forgiving is love," Nola thought to herself.

The next day, Nola told Bexley, "I'm sorry for not forgiving you right away."

"That's okay," Bexley said with a smile. "I'm just so happy I got my best friend back."

"Me, too," said Nola.

Simply Believe

Once upon a time, there was a little boy named Niko who loved to play soccer and wanted to be a star soccer player when he grew up. But there was one little problem. Niko did not believe in himself.

Niko had an older sister named Kia. One day, Kia told Niko, "With your attitude, Niko, you will never be a star soccer player. It's simply simple. You just need to believe in yourself, and then nothing can stop you. Simply believe. You need to practice every day to become better and better."

Kia told Niko to close his eyes and picture himself as a famous soccer player one day.

"Wow!" said Niko. "I really do see myself as a famous soccer player."

"You just need to believe," said Kia. "Practice hard, don't give up, and have confidence. Anything is possible if you simply believe in yourself."

"I'd better go practice," said Niko. "I do simply believe. One day, when I become famous, you will get my first autograph!"

Niko gave his big sister a big hug. They both laughed joyfully.

From that day on, Kia would sometimes even practice soccer with her little brother. With practice and confidence, Niko got a little better every day. That's how simple it is when you believe in yourself.

Without Being Told

"I want to be like a grown-up, just like my sister Priscilla," said little Jeremy. "Then I'll be able to get a puppy, like I've always wanted."

"Then you need to start being responsible," replied Jeremy's daddy.

"Responsible? What does that mean?" Jeremy asked.

"Well, you need to start cleaning your room without being told, just like your big sister," said his daddy. "And you need to put all your toys away without being told."

"What else?" asked Jeremy.

"You should do your homework right after school, without being told."

"Oh," said Jeremy. "So that's what responsibility means? Doing things that need to be done, without being told to do them, just like Priscilla does."

"That's right," said his daddy. "Responsibility helps you become a grown-up."

"Wow!" said Jeremy. "If responsibility will help me grow up, that means I should also get ready for bed and brush my teeth, without being told."

Jeremy did everything that he and his daddy had talked about. On Jeremy's next birthday, when he turned seven, his daddy got him a little puppy. Jeremy was very happy to finally have the pet he had wished for.

"Happy birthday, Jeremy!" said his daddy. "I know you will take very good care of this little puppy, because you have learned that responsibility means doing what needs to be done, without being told."

Two Pounds and Full of Love

There was once a little girl named Lavell, who was six years old. She had a sister named Delia, who was eight years old. Lavell and Delia did not get along. They would fuss about everything. They only got along when it came to Marmalade, their kitten. They just loved Marmalade, and Marmalade loved them back.

Every night, Marmalade would take turns sleeping with one of them. She would put her little paw into one of their hands, and slowly they would fall asleep together.

Marmalade did not like when Lavell and Delia argued, and when they did not listen to their mommy. She would meow and meow at them very loudly, and she made sure that she was heard. Marmalade really wanted the sisters to get along, and to get along with their mommy, too.

One day, after Lavell and Delia had been arguing, Marmalade meowed especially loudly and wouldn't stop.

"What's wrong, Marmalade?" Lavell and Delia asked their kitten.

Marmalade ran off and went under their mommy's bed.

"Come out, Marmalade! Come out!" the girls shouted, but Marmalade did not come out from under the bed.

That night, Marmalade did not sleep with either one of them. Lavell and Delia were sad.

The next morning, they told their mommy what had happened.

"The two of you should try and get along," their mommy told them. "Do it for Marmalade."

Then Lavell and Delia understood that they need to be nice and loving towards each other, because it makes others sad when they argue.

A few days went by, and Marmalade noticed that Lavell and Delia were behaving, and that their mommy was pleased with them for getting along. Marmalade started being her loving self again. She only weighed two pounds, but she was full of love.

Lavell and Delia learned a lot from Marmalade, and did not want to see her unhappy again. Now that they were being kind to one another, they got to sleep with Marmalade's little paw in their hands once more.

My Cozy Little Bed!

Once upon a time, there was a little boy named Boone who loved his cozy little bed and his puppy named Happy. Every night, Boone and Happy would sleep cuddled up together to be warm and cozy.

As the months went by, Happy got bigger and Boone's bed seemed smaller.

"Happy, you got bigger," said Boone. "You should sleep at the end of the bed now." But Happy did not like sleeping at the end of the bed. He liked to sleep close to Boone.

As more months went by, Happy grew into a very big dog, but he still liked to cuddle up with Boone in his cozy little bed.

One night, Boone was frustrated with not having enough space to himself in his own bed.

"Happy, we both cannot fit in my bed," Boone said. "It's not cozy any more. You need to sleep at the end of the bed, or on the rug."

Happy started to whimper.

"Alright, Happy. You can cuddle up with me, but just for one more night," said Boone.

Happy climbed into Boone's cozy little bed, and Boone felt like he was going to fall out of it. But then he turned over and saw Happy's smiling face.

"How could I say no to you?" Boone said. "I know it's nice to share."

The next night, when Boone went to his room at bedtime, there was a new, bigger bed waiting for him, and Happy was sitting happily on top of it, wagging his tail excitedly. Boone jumped into bed with Happy. There was plenty of room for both of them now.

"Thank you, mommy!" Boone shouted joyfully. "I know this was your idea! This is now my cozy big bed with lots of room to share. I love it!"

North Star

Once there was a boy named Dallas, who lived on a little farm with his daddy and his Nana Roxanna. Dallas had wanted a pony for the longest time.

One day, Dallas and his daddy finally went to a bigger farm to pick out a pony to bring home. In one of the paddocks, Dallas noticed a light grey pony that was missing an ear. The pony was looking very sad and lonely, standing all by himself away from the other ponies.

Dallas slowly went up to the pony and looked into his big, beautiful eyes. He could see his reflection in the pony's sad eyes.

"What's wrong, pony?" asked Dallas?

The pony tried to rest his head on Dallas's shoulder, and Dallas gave him a big hug right back. When the farmer saw that, he could hardly believe it.

"North Star has never done that before," he said.

"Is that his name?" asked Dallas

"Yes," said the farmer. "I've had him since he was a foal."

"Why is he standing all alone?" Dallas asked.

"Well, he was born with only one ear," said the farmer. "Nobody wants a pony with only one ear. But it's a shame, because he's a very sweet, quiet pony."

"I want him!" Dallas shouted to his daddy. "I want North Star!"

Dallas and his daddy took North Star home that very day.

When they got home to their little farm, they introduced North Star to Nana Roxanna, and she happily gave him an apple. After enjoying his apple, North Star neighed joyfully.

As the days went by, North Star loved playing with Dallas, and even galloped around after him in the fields.

"You're so kind," Dallas told his pony. "How could anyone not have wanted you? You inspire me to be kind all the time. You really are a bright, shining North Star, and I love you very much."

North Star neighed with happiness. Dallas and North Star slowly settled down in the grass at their favourite spot by a big oak tree, and they took a little nap together.

We hope that you enjoyed these stories!
Be sure to check out our other books too!!

CPSIA information can be obtained
at www.ICGtesting.com
Printed in the USA
BVHW020534240621
610256BV00003B/33